D1101789

THE HIGHWAY MEN

Ken MacLeod

SANDSTONE vista 8

The Sandstone Vista Series

The Highway Men
First published 2006 in Great Britain by Sandstone Press Ltd
PO Box 5725, Dingwall, Ross-shire, IV15 9WJ, Scotland

Sandstone Press gratefully acknowledges the ongoing support
of Highland Council, Highland Adult Literacy Partnership,
and Essex County Council Libraries.

The moral right of the author has been asserted in accordance
with the Copyright, Designs and Patents Act 1988.

ISBN-10: 1-905207-06-9
ISBN-13: 978-1-905207-06-0

The Sandstone Vista Series of books has
been written and skilfully edited
for the enjoyment of readers with differing levels
of reading skills, from the emergent to the accomplished.

Designed and typeset by Edward Garden Graphic Design,
Dingwall, Ross-shire, Scotland.

Printed and bound by Bell and Bain, Glasgow, Scotland.

SANDSTONEPRESS
CONTEMPORARY QUALITY READING

www.sandstonepress.com

To Michael

1. DIAMOND CUTTING

It was Murdo Mac who noticed it first. He was riding shotgun. So he could see farther ahead. I had to keep my eye on the road. First I know of it, Murdo bangs on the cab roof. Signal to stop. I braked gently. The early morning road was icy and treacherous. We were about half a kilometre outside a village a bit out from Dingwall. More a thin straggle of houses, really, like most villages in the Highlands. And like most, it was empty. We knew that.

I rolled down the window. Cold air came in. Murdo poked his head into the cab. His face was red inside the furry parka hood.

'What's up?' I asked.

'There's something no right about yon houses,' he said. 'Can't for the life of me see what it is, though.'

I looked sideways at Euan Campbell. He handed me the binoculars. I propped my elbows on the steering wheel and got the glasses into focus. The five or six houses were on a curve of the road up ahead. I could see all of them. They had that Highland look of being out of place. Like suburban houses stuck down on the moors. Gardens overgrown, sheds falling apart, big bay windows black and empty.

That was it.

'Nae glass in the windows,' I said. 'In *any* of the windows. And it's not broken, either. Just missing.' I passed the binoculars out to Murdo. 'See for yourself.'

He fiddled with the focus wheel. Clumsy in thick gloves. He drew in a sharp breath as he looked.

'That's it,' he said, as he handed the glasses back.

'Not much to go on,' said Euan.

'Doesn't look right,' said Murdo.

'Hunker down,' I said. 'We'll take it slow.'

Murdo's head disappeared from the window. Checking the wing mirror I could see he had ducked back into the lookout's bucket. Shaped like an oil drum, it was bolted to the back of the cab, right behind the driver. It had a low seat, and a roll of armour padding wrapped around the inside. Not very comfortable. We used to take turns.

I eased into first gear and the big Highway truck rolled forward. Three hundred metres. Two hundred. One hundred. The first house had a pair of tall rowans growing at the gap where the gate had been. Couldn't say they had brought much luck. I braked and turned off the engine.

No sound but a blackbird's song and the croak of a hoodie crow up on the hill.

'I'll have a look,' I said. I jumped out of the cab with a thud of wellies and a crackle of oilskins. 'Keep me covered, Murdo.' Even to myself it sounded a bit corny.

'Are we in China or what?' Murdo scoffed.

'It's you that's got us twitchy,' I pointed out.

'Whatever you say, Jase.' Murdo pushed back his parka hood and planted a helmet on his head. The end of the shotgun barrel poked over the rim of the bucket.

I walked up the grassy strip where the path had been. A plastic tricycle, its colours faded, lay in the weeds to one side. I kicked a flat football out of the way and stepped over a broken plant-pot to look at the big window to the right of the door. I glanced inside the room behind the empty window, just to check. A rotting sofa against the far wall, a coffee jar, a mouldy mug. No dangers there. I looked down at the window frame. Above the cracked wood and blistered paint there was maybe half an inch of glass. It was the same all around the frame. The glass had been cut out. I moved to the window on the other side – another empty room, with a plastic chair in the middle of the floor – and found the same. Farther around the house was the wee window of the downstairs toilet. Half an inch of frosted glass along all four sides of it.

I crunched through frosty bracken and nettles, put my foot on the sagging wire of the fence, and hopped into the next empty house. Same deal with the windows.

'Someone's cut out all the glass with a glass cutter,' I said, back at the lorry.

'"With a glass cutter!"' Euan mocked. 'Whatever next?'

'Why would anybody bother?' I asked. 'They

could buy all the glass they wanted in Inverness.'

'To save themselves the drive to Inverness,' said Murdo.

'We're wasting our time here,' said Euan.

'We can spare a minute,' I said. I turned and walked to the fifth house along. It was smaller than the others and had no garden. The front room window was cut out just like the others. In the room was a bedstead up against the back wall. It didn't look like it had been a bedroom. I imagined a sick person lying there, gazing out.

Gazing out. Suddenly it hit me that I'd been looking at this the wrong way. *Really* looking the wrong way. I stepped to the door and pushed. It swung open. Inside I found a narrow hallway with stairs a few steps ahead. There were a lot of scratches on the walls and the banister, and on the floor leading into the room. When I looked through, I saw that the scratches led straight to the legs of the bedstead.

The bedstead had been dragged in. When the floor was bare after the carpets and everything else had been taken from the house.

I sat down on the creaking springs and looked out the empty window. I could see the road and a low dry-stone wall. A patch of overgrown grass on the other side. Then the moor behind it and the hills in the far distance. Long shadows of short fence-posts. That frozen yellow grass across the way would be a sweet green meadow in the spring and summer. The wild sheep would come down from the hills and eat it. Them or the deer. The deer would be way down the hills now, off the moors and into the glens.

'Got ya!' I said to myself. I was out the door and across the road in a minute. I jumped the ditch and the wall into the meadow and searched along the foot of the wall at the far side. I knew what I was looking for, but it was pure luck that I spotted it: a gleam of steel. I bent over and picked up a six-inch bolt with a blunt point at one end. The other end was tapered with four narrow raised bits like low fins along it. It looked like a toy rocket.

A cross-bow bolt.

'The house is a hide,' I said to Euan and Murdo, back at the lorry. 'For maybe a dozen people. They took the windows out, dragged up chairs and couches or whatever and made themselves comfortable, and just sat there waiting for a herd of deer or maybe a flock of sheep to go and eat the grass. The beasts wouldn't see them, wouldn't even smell them. They just had to wait and then let fly with cross-bolts. You could bring down ten at one go that way. Maybe more.'

'Very nice,' said Murdo. I couldn't tell whether he meant my detective work or the killing I had detected.

'Why not just smash out the windows?' said Euan.

'To keep it quiet,' said Murdo.

'From who? The deer?' said Euan.

'Maybe,' I said. I wasn't so sure about that.

'Not much sport in the shooting,' said Euan.

'This was not for sport,' I said.

'Aye,' said Murdo. 'And speaking of food, my breakfast's in Lochcarron, and that's two hours away if we're lucky.'

'Breakfast? What do you call the bacon roll you had in Dingwall?'

'A snack.'

'A midnight feast,' said Euan. 'It was that dark I was expecting to feel my wife.'

'That was just me,' I said. 'You had me worried.'

2. SMOKING GUN

Euan smoked a roll-up before we got back into the cab. Nobody complained. We'd all got kind of easier on him and his bad habit since the big story came out. Maybe it's all been forgotten now, when you're reading this. But you surely must remember the name of Jin Yang.

Jin Yang, right. The guy who started the whole thing. He was a rock music promoter who'd just made his second visit to the Edinburgh Fringe. Great success by all accounts. Real wheeler and dealer, signed up all kinds of acts to play in Beijing. He was on his way home, on a plane just out of Edinburgh Airport. Jumps up while the seat-belt sign's still on, gets into an argument with the trolley dolly. Gets a wee bit physical. He doesn't know that she's had martial arts training. Anti-hijack policy, see? She doesn't know that he is a kung fu master. Things get a bit out of hand and just as he has her in a headlock he gets a soft-nosed bullet in the skull. Turns out there's this plain-clothes cop travelling undercover on the plane. More anti-hijack policy. A sky marshall, as the Americans call them.

So the Chinese guy goes down, and they're all kind of looking at each other. There's blood and bits of bone and brains splattered everywhere. Kids screaming. Adults screaming. Total shock and panic. And the sky marshall sees, right there sticking out of the pocket of the late Mr Yang's seat, a couple of books. They're in Chinese, but they have the titles in English inside. One of them is the Koran. The other is the Selected Speeches of some Chinese leader.

The sky marshall's telling all this to his bosses on the ground, using the plane's own radio. Everybody's hearing him. Then another Chinese passenger a few seats back jumps up and starts yelling. The sky marshall turns to him, with his gun levelled. By this time, half the passengers are telling their folks, using their own mobile phones. They all think they're about to die, and they're right.

Because the wee sign that used to warn you not to use mobiles and so on while the plane was taking off or landing was there for a reason. Your gadgets really can interfere with the aircraft's controls. Well, they did this time anyway. The plane's been called back, obviously. But something goes wrong on its approach. There was a heavy fog that day over the Firth of Forth. Pilot's flying blind. Flying by instruments. Instruments that have been knocked out of kilter by some computer geek's fancy new mobile phone, while he's telling his girlfriend he loves her or what have you.

Controlled flight into terrain, it's called. In this case, the terrain is the naval dockyard at Rosyth. Where Britain's top aircraft carrier is in dock for a refit before a mission to the South China Sea. And in the South China Sea there's been a bit of bother over Taiwan – a breakaway big island that the Chinese are very touchy about.

Kaboom.

A headline the next day says CHINESE AL QAEDA NUKES ROSYTH. And that was *The Guardian*, man. *The Record* just said BOMB REDS NOW.

Most of the British Army was in Iran already. China wasn't exactly a long march away. The Yanks took care of the heavy stuff, as usual. Japan got stuck in too, for no better reason I can see than from force of habit.

Two years into the war our boys were up to their eyebrows in shit. Not knowing where the next attack's coming from – Communists, Muslims, Japanese, you name it.

Meanwhile, the official machinery is grinding away. Government inquiry sifts through the wreckage of the Rosyth incident. Plods through every surviving witness. Brings out a report.

It tells us three important things about Jin Yang.

One – he's from China's Muslim minority. Hence the Koran in the seat.

Two – he's a businessman and a member of the Party. Hence the book of speeches by a Communist official. All about how building up business and getting rich is the way to the glorious future. Jin Yang has to swot up on that sort of thing, and parrot it every now and again to keep his bosses happy.

Three – Jin Yang was a heavy smoker, like lots of Chinese men are. On his first visit to the

Festival Fringe, he had had a very nice time. Deals
in smoke-filled rooms and all that. At the airport
he got through half a pack of cigarettes in the
departure lounge to calm his nerves. There was a
special booth for that very purpose. All's well.
Second time, a good few years later, the smoking
ban had come in. He had a much less fun visit. He
did a lot of his deals in doorways. On his way
home, he's through security and stuck in aeroplane
land when he finds that the smoking booth has
long since been ripped out. His flight's delayed.
Nobody knows just when it'll be ready. Even if he
could get back through security, he's afraid he'll
miss his flight, and then he'll miss his connection.
So he's stuck.

For three and a half hours.

It wasn't a hijack. There was no Al Qaeda
connection. No Chinese government connection
either.

It was just air rage.

So that's how the war started.

And that's why we all stood around quite patient
like and waited for Euan to finish his roll-up
before we got back in the truck for the long drive
to Lochcarron.

3. FRANKENFOLK

We pulled into Lochcarron a couple of hours later. The journey hadn't been bad. The sun glared on the snow when we were up high on the hillsides, but I had good shades. The black ice was murder down in the hollows, but the truck had good tyres. Some new kind of carbon fibre stuff. Their grip was magic. And we didn't run into any bandits or wolves.

'When I was wee the snow would have melted long ago by now,' said Euan. 'Snowline at fifty metres in March! It used to be nearer two hundred.'

Lochcarron was a mile or two out of our way. We passed the end of the road that led away to where we were going to work. That road cut across the head of the sea-loch, towards the old railway line. A mile along it you could see the bright yellow work cabins, and the big black reel that held the cable that snaked out of the water. Lochcarron is a kilometre of houses along the northern shore. This morning the loch was like glass. The long ranges of hills that rose from both shores were mirrored in it like two wavy blades. The hillsides were black with the stumps of trees that had been nipped dead in the Big Freeze and then burned in the forest fires of the next summer. Tall windmills stood along the hills' snow-covered tops. If any of the blades were turning at all it was too slow to see. Some of the windmill pylons were leaning over. Others lay flat on their sides. I remember when wind-power farms were the next big thing. The wind had other ideas.

I slowed the big truck as we came in, past the grassy patch that used to be a golf course and the walled patch that's still a cemetery. Around the side of a hill to the village proper. The brown stones and grey pebble-dash of the old houses were mixed in with the bright colours of the new ones. Blue, pink, yellow, green. They looked more like machines than buildings. Pipes and aerials sprouted from them. Thick insulating mats covered their walls. Steep roofs jutted up like witches' hats. The roofs of the old houses were covered with solar-power tarps.

The hotel was one of the old buildings. Crumbling concrete patched with insulating mats. Not much of a hotel now. More of a coffee shop and pit-stop. A couple of supply trucks and two or three small cars were filling up, with red power cables and green bio-fuel lines plugged into their sides. Behind the thick plastic of the front window the cafe was busy. I parked around the side – our fuel cells were still well charged and the bio-fuel tank was half full. The three of us trooped in. Warm air smelling of coffee steam and frying bacon. About a dozen people sat around the tables. As usual everybody stared at us. It's these big yellow boiler suits with HIGHWAY on front and back that does it. Dead giveaway. I was still throwing back my hood and unzipping the front of my overall when I heard the first nasty remark. One of the guys whose lorry was recharging outside – I could see that by the Tesco jacket on the back of his chair – leaned over and said to the Fed-Ex driver he shared the table with:

'Laggers. Too dumb tae draft.'

Coming from a trucker, that was a bit rich. I

ignored it. I didn't retort with: 'Truckers. Too feart tae fight.' I just strolled to the counter and ordered a pot of java and six bacon rolls.

Thing is, it would have been true. You can dodge the draft by being a truck driver. But the trucker was right and all. Except that we *are* drafted. Only not for the Army. The Army needs people who can handle high tech. Just the same as civilian industries, all that Carbon Glen stuff. People who were good at school. The rest of us – those who can't or won't hack it as soldiers or high tech workers – get swept up by the Highway. There's no going on the dole or the sick these days. It's my way or the Highway, like the First Minister used to say.

Of course it's not just building roads any more. The old Highways Department took over all the public works. One of them was insulation. Lagging pipes was the first emergency job. Loads of insulation had to be laid on in the last summer before the first Big Freeze. That's why all of us who work for the Highway are called laggers. Well, it's one reason. The other is that 'lagger' used to be the swear word for people like us. It came into fashion just after 'neds' went out.

Not that I mind. I always wanted to be a lagger. Ever since I was about eight years old, anyway. That was when some new plastic water mains were laid in the street round the corner. Me and my wee gang were tearaways. We weren't as bad as folks said we were. OK, we did break all the windows of the JCB digger one night. But we thought the guys who laid the pipes were great. They had yellow plastic helmets and bright yellow plastic waistcoats and big muddy boots. They looked tough. They looked like we might want to be like when we grew up. Them and fighter pilots and the characters in Grand Theft Auto. Guess what. You need university to be a fighter pilot. Two of my pals died five years later doing Grand Theft Auto in real life. Handbrake turns don't work so well on country roads. Funny that.

Anyway.

Apart from the truckers the other people in the room giving us the eye were locals. Five natives and five incomers. The natives were in their usual suspicious huddle. They just gave us a long enough glance to figure out we weren't about to attack them. Then they turned away. Their backs were about as welcoming as rolled-up hedgehogs.

Four of the white settlers sat in a more relaxed way around another table. Two couples, I guessed. English accents, or maybe posh Scottish.

' – so then Malcolm sold his flat in the New Town and bought – '

Sudden pause. They looked at us, and then they looked down their noses. On the bridge of each of these noses was a black squiggle, like the bottom half of a glasses frame. The latest gadget from Carbon Glen. It seemed our faces weren't online anywhere as bad guys, because the incomers all looked up and blinked and went on talking.

' – she's still with the World Trade Organization, and she's very worried – '

This checking us out stuff was as much of an insult as what the trucker had said. One look at *their* faces told me they'd had the Reverse treatment. It's supposed to turn back the clock, but it doesn't. Not quite. Smoothes out the skin and tightens up the muscles. Helps the bones and joints too, I'm told. But it never wipes away all the signs of age. It's illegal in Scotland, because it does things to your genes. There's laws against

GM *crops*, for crying out loud. GM *people* are an even bigger no-no. But what few cops there are in the Highlands are too busy – or have too much sense – to hunt down Frankenfolk. Place is crawling with them.

The woman behind the counter, a broad-in-the-beam local who for sure had not had the Reverse treatment, was still tonging strips of bacon into rolls so fresh I could smell them, when I noticed the fifth incomer checking us out.

This lassie was a crustie. Her black hair was in matted braids. Her face was not bad and had been washed in the last day or two. Over the back of her chair was a hide jacket. She wore a shapeless woollen sweater. Long legs in some kind of tweedy tartan trousers. Feet in buckle-sided boots propped on a plastic chair. She was sitting at a small table by herself, over by the window around the side of the counter. She had a white teapot and a cup of green tea in front of her. Beside them on the table was a scatter of pages printed off from the day's papers.

She looked us up and down in a lazy way and then looked back at her papers. When we sat down at the empty table beside her she paid us no attention. She did swing her legs off the chair and lean forward over the off-prints. I could smell her. It wasn't a stink. Sweat and wool and something like the sea.

Finished the bacon roll and on to my second coffee. I was fiddling with the cross-bolt, turning it over my fingers. We were talking about the day's job when I felt a stare on my neck. I turned and saw the lassie looking hard at me, then down at my hands. No, she was looking at the thing in my hands. Then she looked away. She shrugged into her big jacket, picked up a bulging carrier bag, stood up and walked out.

4. AILISS

'Nice ass,' said Euan.

'Well boys,' I said when we'd watched her out, 'about time we did the same.'

'Not walking like that,' said Euan, getting back at me.

I nodded to agree we were evens. Euan was already rolling his cigarette. He wagged his tongue back and forth against his top lip. One up to him.

'Move your arse,' I told him. 'You can go shotgun. Smoke all you want.'

I couldn't be sure if this was one up to me.

As we drove back up the street we saw the girl from the cafe trudging along the side of the road. The Tesco bag was weighing her down on one side. I slowed the truck and wound down the cab window.

'Want a lift?'

The girl opened her mouth and said something. Out of the corner of my eye I saw two hurtling shapes, black and spiky as ninja knives. As my head whipped round to follow them I saw them skimming above the loch at about twenty metres. The sound of the fighter jets hammered over us a moment after they'd disappeared.

'What?' I asked.

'I said, "Where are you heading?"'

'Strathcarron way,' I said.

'Fine,' she said. She crossed the road and walked around the front of the truck. Murdo opened the door and moved over and squashed into the middle seat. The girl stepped up and swung in. She put the bag down between her boots and slammed the door. As she turned back with a smile and a thank you her hair flicked and I could see she didn't have a phone on her ear.

I let the engine's flywheel bite again and released the brake. We slid forward out of the village. I glanced sideways. Murdo was wrinkling his nose. I didn't mind the smell at all.

'What's your name?' I asked.

'Ailiss,' she said, looking ahead and around

like a kid at the front of the top deck of a bus.

'I'm Jase,' I said. 'This is Murdo.'

'You're not from here,' she said.

I could just about tell she was. Her accent was a bit like Euan's.

'I'm from Glasgow,' I said. 'Murdo's from Stornoway.'

'The Highway comes from all over,' Murdo announced. 'You don't look like a native yourself.'

'I was born in Strome,' she said. She jerked a thumb over her shoulder. 'Five miles down the road.'

'A white settler of the second generation,' said Murdo.

'You know a lot about me, don't you?' she said.

'I do that,' said Murdo. 'You have – '

I knew what he was going to say next. I was glad he was close enough to give him the dig of my elbow.

'What?' he said.

'Don't bug the lassie,' I said.

'I was just making conversation.'

'Aye, well make it different.' I kept my eyes on the road. 'Sorry about that, Ailiss.'

She flicked a hand. 'No problem.' She turned to Murdo. 'You're right, my parents were from down south. They were just so typical, they collected pine resins for aromatherapy ...' She went on about this for a bit.

But I could see where her hand went while she spoke, maybe without her even thinking about it. It went to her knee, then crept to the top of her boot.

'I live past Strathcarron,' she said, as I slowed at the turn-off.

'Fine,' I said. 'We'll drop you at the site. You'll have to walk or hitch from there.'

'I'll walk,' she said.

'Not far to go then?' said Murdo. Still prying.

'Not far at all,' she said. 'Up behind Strathcarron.'

Now I know for a fact there's nothing up behind Strathcarron. There's nothing *at* Strathcarron, except the old railway station, some empty houses and the ruins of a restaurant. Up the hills behind it there's waste howling wilderness. It was empty even before the freeze. There's bugger all people between here and Kintail. Bugger all beasts for that matter. You'd be hard pressed to find enough dead sheep to feed a crow.

I kept my trap shut about all this and I glared at Murdo to do the same.

We crossed the Carron bridge and pulled up just before the site road end, two or three hundred metres from the old station.

'Thanks,' said Ailiss. She hopped out, hauled her bag after her, waved, shut the door and strode off along the road. The end of the loch was to her right and the site to her left. She didn't look to either side, or back.

'Well,' said Euan as he climbed down from the lookout bucket to the running-board, 'there goes a girl who is not afraid of bandits.'

Murdo and I both laughed.

'What?' said Euan. He handed the shotgun in through the cab window. I clipped it to the rack behind the seats.

'She's armed,' I said. 'At least a knife, and maybe a gun as well. And she lives up in the hills behind Strathcarron.' I waved at the range in front of us.

'And she has no food in that bag,' said Murdo, 'except some sugar and a packet of Rich Abernethy biscuits. It's all stuff like batteries and disinfectants.'

'What's that got to do with it?' demanded Euan.

I started the engine again and began the turn, over an earth-covered culvert and on to the site. As the security guard waved a scanner at us I glanced up the road for traffic. There was none. The girl was a couple of hundred metres away, walking fast.

'She's a bandit,' I said.

5. SITE WORK

We had brought a Caterpillar digger on the back of the truck. Getting it off was hard work. Our thick gloves made the chains awkward to handle, but they were too cold to touch with bare skin. The heavy padlocks and hasps were frozen solid. It took a lot of tapping with a hammer to get them loose. The tailgate ramps were stiff. We had to melt ice off them with a blowtorch before Euan could drive the Cat down to the ground. He had just eased the tracks over the edge of the flatbed and was inching forward, waiting to tip forward on to the slope of the ramps, when I saw a black cloud in the west. Way down the loch. By the time the Cat was on the ground you couldn't see Lochcarron.

I looked around. It was weird to be standing in bright sunshine with that black wall of cloud on the way. All over the site – there were about twenty guys working there – people were yelling, hauling tarpaulins over equipment, shutting down machinery, and running for shelter. Only the guards stood their ground. Their armour would take more than a storm to damage.

'Time to go, boys,' I said.

Euan jumped out of the Cat and locked the door behind him. Murdo pulled his parka hood up and headed for the nearest depot. I heaved the two boards one by one into the back of the truck and banged the tailgate up, slammed the bolts across.

I could hear a hissing from the sea a couple of hundred metres away.

I ran after Euan towards the doorway where Murdo was standing among a crowd of others, staring past us and waving. Beckoning, urging us on. A gust of wind pushed us like a giant hand on our backs. The hiss became a drumming roar. We had just got under the roof when hailstones the size of golf balls started hitting the tarmac. They hit so hard they shattered. I felt a sting of ice on my face, and covered my eyes. Everybody backed further inside, pressing against machines and tools and coils of pipe.

For ten minutes it was almost as dark as night. The ground in front of us turned slowly white. The hailstones hammered on the roof. I could see them bouncing off the side window of the depot and wondered why it didn't break. Then I remembered it was probably made of toughened glass, just like the truck windscreen and the Cat's cabin windows. This thought reminded me of something, but I couldn't think what. With all the noise I could hardly think at all.

Then the hailstorm passed as suddenly as it had started. The sky was still overcast, and the wind fresh, but the squall had marched off up the glen. We walked out, boots crunching on chunks of ice.

'The ground needed it,' said Euan.

'Yes indeed, it'll be good for the crops,' said Murdo.

'Aye, the spring sowing needs it,' I said.

We went on with this farming talk until it stopped being funny. That didn't take long.

I led the way to the yellow dome of the site office. A local lassie looked at us from behind a desk as we trooped in.

'Site engineer?' I asked.

'He'll be back in a minute,' she said.

'OK,' I said.

Her hands were moving on the keyboard but she was watching the news. It scrolled down a screen tacked to the wall beside a calendar. March was a bare girl on a wet rock somewhere hot. April would be a hot girl on a bare rock somewhere wet. On the screen the top news was a Siberian town that had sunk two metres overnight. They're thawing while we're freezing. Russian kids in army uniforms helped folk into long trucks with huge fat wheels. The rest of the news was the usual. Truck-bomb in Tehran. Ambush in Kabul.

'The Bodach's been busy,' said Euan.

The Bodach – the old man – is what the locals call Osama Bin Laden. Nobody knows if he's still alive or not. Maybe he's getting the Reverse treatment but he's not in a healthy line of work. His gloating videos still come out every now and again. But that doesn't prove anything. You could say the same about Mick Jagger.

A man in a suit and wellies hurried in with that look of someone who has just been for a pee. His belt was one notch too tight for his belly and his thinning hair had been flattened by twenty-odd years under hard hats. Red cheeks and sandy eyebrows and sharp blue eyes.

'Liam Morrison,' he said, shaking hands.

'We've brought the Cat,' I said after we'd introduced ourselves.

'Good,' he said. He ambled to the desk and pawed at loose paper. 'The chart, Kelly?'

'It's in here somewhere,' she said. 'Got it.'

Over by the curved wall a printer whizzed. Kelly got up and came back with a metre of paper. Liam looked around for somewhere to spread it, then held it up against the wall.

'That's your line for the trench,' he said. 'It's all marked out on the ground. From the river to the railway. Yellow posts and green string, mind. The red one's for the site sewage line.'

We peered at the drawing and got this clear in our heads.

'OK,' I said.

'You better take it,' said Liam. 'Don't get it wet.'

We all laughed and Liam nodded and we headed out.

'"Don't get it wet,"' Euan muttered.

'Taking the piss,' I said. 'But he's polite for

a boss.'

'The gentleman will have his little joke,' said Murdo.

Lack of water was what had brought us here in the first place. The hailstorm was the usual way water falls from the sky around here. Not much of that, and not much rain, not even much snow. The rain that does fall comes in heavy bursts that run off in flash floods. The snow that does fall, up on the tops, doesn't melt near soon enough. The Highlands are drying out. So the Hydro stations that kept the Highlands lit up in the old days don't get enough water to work. Wind power turned out to be a crock as soon as the weather went wild. It's either so calm the blades don't turn or so stormy the pylons get blown over.

So here we were, climbing on to the Cat and getting ready to dig a trench to hold a cable. One end of the cable was coiled up on the bank of the Carron. The rest of it ran out along the riverbed and across the tidal flat and along the bottom of the loch. All the way out to the new nuclear power station on a wee island between the mouth of Loch Carron and the Isle of Skye. The wee island is called Eilean Mor, which means Big

Island. The power station was built on it because nobody lives there to object, and also because it's easy to guard. In the Sound of Skye there's enough military and naval hardware to scare off the Bodach himself.

The first part of our job was to dig a trench from the Carron to the back of the old railway station. The railway line was a ready-made route across country to Loch Luichart. At Loch Luichart, about twenty kilometres inland, was one of those dry Hydro power stations I told you about. Somebody had decided that this would be just the place to plug the new power into the grid. It had all the machinery, but it was lying idle.

The trains don't run any more on the Kyle line – too many landslides – so the rails were free to carry heavy equipment. Any day now the machine would come chugging down from Inverness. Then it would slowly chug back, digging a trench alongside the railway track as it went. Same trick for laying the cable. All we'd have to do was follow behind and shovel the dirt in, and lay prefab concrete covers over any stretches where the cable had to be trailed over bare rock.

All very straightforward. But first we had to

dig this trench through a couple hundred metres of soil that was on the way to freezing solid. Tomorrow's permafrost. And the day after tomorrow's swamp, if Alaska and Siberia are anything to go by. But that's the day after tomorrow's problem.

Liam Morrison had done his bit with the theodolite and laser gadget. His two assistants (I could see from the names on the drawing) had done their thing with sticks and string. The line they'd marked out for the trench to follow stretched straight from the Carron's left bank to just east of the station. Easy.

Our only instruction was to dig a metre deep all the way along it. By the time Murdo had got the Cat to the side of the river we were lined up and ready to go. Point and shoot.

Nothing's ever that simple.

6. WARNING LABEL

The Cat was so new you could still see yellow and black paint that had never had dust on it. It was a new model and all. It had a big chain winch. It had a drill attached to the digger scoop. Beside the drill was the nozzle of a heat blaster, hose-piped to the engine, for thawing frozen ground.

So why was I down in the trench with a pick and spade and crowbars? Why were we only fifty metres along, towards the end of the second day after we'd arrived?

I was asking these questions not very politely.

'It's the Ice Age, man,' Euan explained, leaning on a shovel, holding a chain, smoking a tab, and offering advice from above. 'The glaciers left a lot of boulders when they went.'

'At this rate,' I said, wedging the end of a

crowbar behind one of said boulders, 'they'll be here when the glaciers come back.'

'Not long to wait then,' said Murdo, from behind the levers in the cab.

'Pass me the flexies,' I said.

Euan flung the chain rattling down. On the end of it was a bunch of cables made from some fancy carbon tech. These were the flexies. If you stretched any two of them out, wrapped them around something then brought the ends together they could writhe like snakes into a knot. This was a fix for exactly the problem we had right now: buried boulders. (As well as for tree stumps and stuck cars and stuff like that.)

The trouble was you had to have enough clear space around your obstacle to wrap them in. I heaved on the crowbar. The boulder rocked a few centimetres. Soil that had been hard even for the drill to break into suddenly crumbled and slid into the gap. It filled it completely. I heaved again. I knew this could be done. We'd done it about twenty times already. People had been growing oats and potatoes and turnips on this plain for hundreds of years. You'd think they'd have got rid of all the boulders. Turns out they only got rid of them as deep as the plough digs, which is not a metre, not even half a metre.

'Why don't you just take the trench around the boulders?' Liam had asked. He moved his hand like a fish.

'You know what we find when we do that?'

'Other boulders?'

'Got it.'

'Oh well. Carry on, gentlemen.'

So we carried on. My second heave on the crowbar shifted the boulder again. I could see black space behind it.

'Give us a hand,' I said.

Euan spat his tab and jumped down into the trench and wrapped a pair of flexies around the boulder. The ends knotted themselves. At the same time tiny grippers came out the cable and stuck to the rock like ivy. I let the crowbar sag back. We stood and looked at it for a minute.

'It'll no hold,' I said. 'It's too near the top.'

Euan stretched five more flexies across the exposed surface, then tugged on the chain.

'It'll stick like an octopus to a face-mask,' he proclaimed.

'Well, I'm not sticking around,' I said.

We clambered out of the trench, backed well clear, and gave Murdo the thumbs up. The winch whined. The chain straightened. The tension built. The chain and flexies lashed through the air like a cat-o'-nine-tails and clanged against the cab.

'So much for that,' said Euan. 'Try again?'

I looked around. The sun was behind the Atlantic. To the east the pink sky was making the cut-out face of a giant of the mountain. The one the locals call Wellington's Nose.

'Call it a day,' I said.

We washed up, and had some grub in the canteen. Then we cadged a lift for the hotel bar from an Iraqi refugee on work placement who was keen to make friends. Thank God for Muslims. Well, on-side Muslims anyway, if you see what I mean. They don't complain about having to drive back from the pub. I stood the first round and bought a tall orange juice for young Farhad and a half and a half each for myself and the lads. The whisky bottles all had labels showing the diseased liver of the month. The beer mats showed a range of car crash injuries. The bar had been built like a conservatory. Its big windows had long since been sprayed over with insulation foam. Too mean or too poor even for double glazing. The light was yellow. There was a score or so of people here, usual mix of local soaks and less sozzled incomers. Couple of other teams from the site. Most of the crew preferred to drink in the barracks. No smoke detectors hot-linked to the local cop shop, for one thing. Better atmosphere in every way, you could say. People had stopped staring at us after the first night. I stared at them on my way back to the table with the tray.

'Looking for somebody?' Euan asked.

'He's pining for his bandit,' said Murdo.

This was true but I denied it. I had found Ailiss on my mind the past couple of days. I had been keeping an eye out for her, but I hadn't seen her on the road or in the village.

'I meant to ask,' said Euan. 'Why did you call her a bandit?'

Farhad looked worried. 'You have bandits here?'

'Just a few rebels in the hills,' said Murdo.

'Don't wind up the kid,' I told him, then turned to Farhad. 'They're no like your Kurds or anything. They're just small groups of young folks mostly who live up in the mountains. They call themselves new age settlers. Some of them do a bit of stealing. One or two of them sometimes even hold up a supply lorry on a lonely road. That's why they get called bandits.'

'But why do they do it?' asked Farhad.

I shrugged. 'To get stuff.'

'No, I mean why do they live in the mountains?'

'To get away from' – I waved a hand around – 'all this.'

I didn't know what I meant, what I was waving my hand at. It was the warning labels and the smoke detectors and the CCTV cameras. Or it was the hard-drinking locals and the smug incomers. Or maybe the yammering telly, and the horrible thick air of the place, smelling of sweat and scent and food and booze. The yellow light and the blanketed windows. That and the whole shit deal of being a lagger.

Farhad still looked puzzled. 'Immorality?'

'Aye, that's it,' said Murdo. 'Immorality and drunkenness.'

At closing time we stepped out into a black

night full of stars. No many lights to compete with here. From the hills to the south, across the loch, a faint spark rose and climbed fast up the sky. Almost overhead it flared bright for a second or two and then winked out.

'What was that?' I asked.

'The Space Station,' said Murdo.

'It was abandoned,' I said.

'Yes,' said Murdo, 'but it's still up there.'

'The Chinks put a man on Mars before the war,' said Euan.

'Two men and a woman,' Farhad said, opening the van door.

'Maybe they're still up there and all,' Murdo said.

'Aye,' I said. 'With a soldering iron and a sewing machine. Making stuff to sell us after the war.'

'"After the war,"' Euan mocked.

'When I was a wee boy,' said Murdo, 'I heard people saying that.'

When we got back to the site I stopped by the computer and applied for a day off. Nothing came up until Sunday, so I took that.

7. THE BLACK HILLS

The site was quiet on Sunday, though I doubt many went to church. I walked out the gate on a fine crisp morning. Blue sky, blue loch. Flat calm. There was a line or two running in my head from one of my father's old songs: *take me back to the black hills, the black hills of ...*

The black hills of Lochcarron. Oh aye.

My hand was fiddling with the cross-bolt, still deep in my parka pocket, clinking against some change and a knife. A cat hissed at me from an empty window of the old station, making me jump. Behind all the other smells from the ruin – wet ash, cat piss, mould and weeds – there was the faint whiff of disinfectant. Left by a hundred years of soaking the floorboards with it. It reminded me of school corridors and the Highway offices.

I crossed the rusty tracks and found a fallen gate among sagging fenceposts. An overgrown path led up into the hills. I followed it. I was glad of my big boots. The grass hid slippery stones that could turn an ankle, no bother. On the lower slopes I saw a few rabbits and here and there a huddled flock of sheep that had gone wild. These feral sheep looked fierce and alert, with thick wool and long legs. Not like farm sheep at all. Evolution happens, man, whatever the Yanks say. Each flock was guarded by a black-faced ram with yellow eyes that stared at me as I went past. It was like being watched by Satan.

Every so often I looked back, taking in the view. After a bit the curve of the hills hid the loch. I was up above the snowline in a world of black and white. Frost and old snow and burnt heather. There was colour in only a few places. Orange lichens on the rocks like spilled paint. A few green shoots in a warm patch that caught the sun most of the day and where water dripped from icicles on to the brown clumps of dead grass.

By ten o'clock I'd passed a couple of tiny frozen lochs and was walking along a wee glen.

There were hills to my right and left. Higher hills filled the horizon ahead. The place is called the Attadale Forest. Like most places called forests in the Highlands, it has no trees. Nothing grows higher than the heather. The path had faded to a track that might have been made by sheep. There were no sheep up this high, but the path had been trodden not long ago. And that meant people. I was on the right track, you might say.

I wasn't worried about wolves or bears. Back along the big glen of the Carron they could be a problem, but not here. Not in this barren land. Even though Attadale and Glen Affric a bit to the south were among the places they'd been brought back to years ago. It was a big thing back then, around the same time as wind power. Failed for the same reason, too. Climate change. Everybody thinks of wolves in the Highlands but it's down south they're more of a nuisance. In Glasgow they raid the bins.

On and up I went. After a bit I began to find clues that the path was made by people after all. Stones stacked by the side to make a low wall, or spread out along a metre or two that was soft underfoot.

A wisp of smoke stained the sky ahead of me. I sniffed the air and smelled burning wood, with an odd chemical taste in the smell.

I climbed a slope that opened on to a dip overlooked by a high, steep hill. I stopped and stared.

A frozen loch lay at the bottom of the hollow. Alongside it was a row of low buildings. The nearest was like an old black house, with dry-stone walls. Its thatched roof was covered with a solar-power tarp. The tarp was weighed down with boulders hanging from ropes at the corners. The smoke was coming from the chimney of that house. The next building was a long greenhouse. Then another black house, and another greenhouse. Behind them all were some sheds, with stone walls and turf roofs, again with the power tarps. More power tarps were laid along the tops of chicken runs. A couple of scrawny tethered goats grazed the side of the hill.

I had just about time to take this in when I heard a whirring sound and a loud click. Something moved at the corner of my eye and I turned. A little kid had popped up from behind a boulder. He was aiming a crossbow at me.

I held my hands away from my sides.

'Put that down,' I said.

He kept the weapon aimed with one hand. It was a bit shaky but not shaky enough for me to jump him. With his free hand he reached inside his parka and pulled out a whistle. He blew hard on it. The blast rang in my ears even after it had stopped echoing from the hills.

'Don't try anything funny,' he said, trying to sound tough. It just made his voice higher.

'I can give you a spare bolt for that,' I said.

Doors banged and people came running from the buildings. I caught sight of sudden movements on the hillside, just black specks moving and vanishing.

Three people ran up the path and stopped behind the boy. Two bearded guys, and Ailiss.

'Hi, Ailiss,' I said.

'You know this guy?' said Beard Number One. He didn't sound pleased.

'I've met him,' she said. She frowned at me. 'Jase?'

'That's me,' I said.

'He's one of the laggers,' she said.

'What brings you here?' asked Beard Number

Two. He had an English accent.

I shrugged. 'Just out for a walk. My day off.'

'The Sabbath,' said Ailiss, like she'd just remembered something funny. 'Oh well. No harm in that.'

'Would you ask the kid to stop pointing that thing?' I said.

'Yeah,' she said. 'Pack it in, Nichol.'

The kid scowled but did as he was told. He lowered the crossbow and wound the cable back.

'This is not clever,' I said. 'You can't go threatening everybody who walks past.'

'We don't,' said Ailiss. 'Not usually. We're all just a wee bit jumpy.'

'Aye, you can say that again,' I said. I had no idea why they should be jumpy. 'Well, I don't like having things pointed at me.'

'I thought you might be a bandit,' Nichol said. 'Or a refugee or a soldier.'

Beard Number One looked awkward. 'Kids pick things up,' he said.

'Come down to the house and have some tea,' said Ailiss.

I guessed they were trying to make up for the bad welcome.

'Thanks,' I said. 'I could do with that.'

The kid walked beside me down the track.

'What sort of a name is Jase?' he asked.

'Short for something,' I said.

'What?'

'Jason,' I said.

'No a bad name.'

'It is if your second name's Mason.'

'Jason Mason, Jason Mason,' he chanted.

'Not so loud,' I said.

'How will you pay for my silence?' he demanded grandly.

'You been watching too much telly?'

'No telly,' he said. 'I read a lot though.'

I took the cross-bolt out of my pocket and waved it in front of him. 'Will this keep you quiet?'

'Aye, sure.'

I handed it to him.

'Thanks,' he said. He held it up and skipped ahead, shouting: 'Look what I got from Jason Mason!'

Kids.

8. THE GREEN PLACE

The kid turned around and sauntered back up the path to where he'd been, giving me a nod on the way. The two guys and Ailiss led me to the front door of the first house. We all ducked through the low doorway. They were burning broken planks and other scrap timber in the fireplace. Some of it had paint or varnish. That was what gave it the chemical smell. But it was a cheery enough fire and there was a pot of tea on the hob. I took it black and strong with sugar. Nobody offered me a biscuit and I didn't ask. The bearded guys told me their names. Martin and Angus. I guessed they were in their twenties and wondered why they hadn't been drafted. They looked and sounded bright enough for the army. I didn't ask. I sipped tea and looked around.

The bulb hanging from the ceiling was off, so

all the light came from the window. The furniture was burst armchairs and a sagging sofa and an old dresser and chest of drawers. Carpets and rugs lay thick on the floors and more were nailed to the walls. The wall carpets had pictures and clippings and postcards tacked to them. A lot of the pictures looked like they had been printed off the net. Lush green landscapes – you know, historical, like. Trees and flowers, birds and bees. Across other nails banged into the wall were three crossbows, a shotgun higher up, and a couple of air rifles. Tins of pellets and bolts, a box of cartridges on a shelf. The box was brown and waxy, old fashioned. All from before they were banned, I guessed. They sure weren't robbed from the Highway's armouries, or the cops.

No telly, like the kid had said. And no wireless internet that I could see. But books, on paper I mean, were stacked against every wall. You would think they were part of the insulation.

A colder-looking kitchen through at the back. The water pipes were lagged with bits of old carpet tied on with string. Rusty pick and spade and mattock were propped by the sink. A scythe hung on the wall. I pointed to it.

'What's the use of that?'

Ailiss peered. 'Oh, the scythe.' She smiled. 'It'll have a use. There'll be crops again. Oats are hardy. There's a field or two of them run wild.'

'Ailiss is an optimist,' said the Sassenach beardie one. He sounded annoyed for some reason. He shrugged. 'We found it, that's all. Ailiss thinks of uses for it.'

Ailiss gave him a look like she'd just thought of another one. But after that they all glanced at each other and at me and smiled like Mormons.

'Would you like to show him around, Ailiss?' said Angus, the Scottish guy. 'Martin and I have to get back to work. We'll meet up at the other end.'

'See you, guys,' Ailiss said.

They zipped up their parkas, flipped up their hoods and ducked out the door. I drained the mug.

'Well,' said Ailiss, looking a bit awkward, 'let me show you around, Jason Mason.'

'Jase,' I said.

'OK,' she said. She took me out the back door. The back of the house was dug out of the side of the hill. Ailiss turned left and led me along the narrow walled gulley, past a meat-safe that smelled of more than meat.

'Goat cheese,' Ailiss said, when I wrinkled my nose.

'Did youse build all this?' I asked.

She glanced back. 'Just the greenhouses. Not the black houses. They had just the walls left when we found them, mind you.'

'How many of you live here?'

This time she didn't look back. 'No telling.'

'That's me told.'

She laughed. Didn't explain.

But she showed me everything. The greenhouse had tomatoes and other vegetables growing in it, with herbs between the rows. Water from pipes trickled everywhere, warmed by the sun and the solar power. There was even a few square metres of spuds. Fertiliser came from rabbits and goats in the sheds up the back. Other meat – venison from deer and mutton from feral sheep – hung in a cold smoke-hut or soaked in salt barrels. In the second house I met Nichol's parents, who were stitching animal skins with fishing line on a manual sewing machine. They just looked up and didn't say much. Along our whole way I saw maybe half a dozen other people come and go from the hills, some with bits of wood, some with shot rabbits. None of them did more than give me a hard look.

'All that toughened glass must have cost a bomb,' I said, in the second greenhouse.

'Got it from abandoned houses,' Ailiss said. Just as I'd guessed, way back.

'Diamond cutters are handy wee things,' I said. 'And an empty house makes a good hide.'

'Oh, you saw that?'

'Aye, on the road from Dingwall. How did you lug all the meat back?'

She shrugged. 'Borrowed a car.'

Borrowed, aye right. I said nothing.

'No, it really was borrowed,' she said. 'We did that job with some other new settlers from over in the Black Isle.'

She was standing very close, her strange salty smell all mixed up with the fresh air of earth and plants.

'Ailiss,' I said.

She was about to reply when the greenhouse door opened and the two beardie guys, Martin and Angus, walked in. Ailiss took a step back, bumping her hip on a plant-pot. She muttered and turned away to scoop the soil and the plant back in. Martin and Angus half sat on the edge of a trestle table.

'Well,' says Angus, 'you've seen our place.'

'Aye, I have, thank you,' I said. 'Nice place you've got. I'm not sure why you live like this, though.'

Angus looked sideways at Martin. Martin stood up and leaned forward a bit. He clasped his hands behind his back and jutted his beard.

'Survival,' he said. 'The world is going down the tubes. The American grain belt is being hoovered up by tornadoes. The ice is melting everywhere it used to be and freezing where it wasn't. The oil's running out, and we're deep in a war that could go nuclear at any moment. The Greenland ice is about to slide into the sea. One way or another, the cities are doomed. We're living the way everyone will have to live, sooner or later.'

'What a load of shite,' I said.

'What?' he said. He looked a bit staggered.

'Youse just *like* living like this. Fair enough. Don't kid on you're going to survive whatever's coming down. Not unless you can hand-weave solar tarps and make steel for your crossbows and all that. No tae mention the way the wind blows.'

Martin looked like he was just catching up with me. 'What do you mean?'

I pointed. 'From the west. And what's sitting west of here? A nuclear power station and the biggest collection of nuclear missiles since Rosyth blew up. If that lot start flying youse are going down with the rest of us, except maybe faster.'

'Now look here – ' Angus began. Martin waved a hand.

'There's nothing to say,' he said. 'It's pointless arguing with people like that.'

'Fine,' I said. 'I'll shove off. Thanks for the tea.' I looked over my shoulder from the door. 'See you down the village sometime, Ailiss.'

'Maybe,' she said. She looked away. 'Bye.'

9. SUNDAY NIGHT

I was halfway back down the track when I got a call from Murdo asking where the hell I was. I told him I was walking up in the hills and was on my way down. He told me I was an idiot. I told him he wasn't my mother and hung up. But I enjoyed the rest of the walk and I got back to the site about mid-afternoon. I had a late lunch of pork pie and a tin of beer. I went to my bunk in the laggers' hut, kicked off my boots and stretched out for some Sabbath kip.

In the canteen at seven there was only a handful of us there, me and Murdo and Farhad and Kelly the secretary and Liam the site engineer. We all sat at the same table with our microwaved dinners.

'Did you find your bandit?' Murdo asked.

'Aye,' I said. 'They have a wee place up behind

Attadale.'

'Get anywhere with her?'

'Would I be here if I had?' I said.

Murdo laughed.

Liam put down his fork and looked over at me.

'What's this about bandits?'

'They're no bandits,' Murdo said, before I could get a word in. 'Just poachers and tinkers.'

'All the same,' said Liam. 'Let's hear what Jase has to say about it.'

I told him about the settlement, leaving out all the awkward moments.

'That's worrying,' he said.

'What's worrying about it?'

'An armed gang living a few klicks from our power line? That doesn't worry you?'

'Aw come on,' I said. 'They're no threat to anybody. And anyway, there's new age settlers dotted all over the place. All along the glen, for a start.'

Liam nodded. 'Exactly. We haven't taken this seriously enough. It's a security risk.'

'It is no!' I said. 'Why would they want to damage the power line anyway? They think the whole world's going to hell in a handcart already, without them helping it along.'

'Groups with these kinds of beliefs can turn very ugly,' Liam said. 'End of the world cults don't always just wait for the end, you know. Sometimes they try to bring it on. Or they get influenced or' – he paused, and jabbed with his finger – 'mixed up with more militant types.'

Murdo laughed loud. 'Yon tinks might end up working for the Bodach?'

'Or some other extremists, yes,' Liam said. 'Whether they knew it or not.'

I lost my appetite all of a sudden.

'They're not a cult,' I said, 'and they're no extremists either. They're just' – I shrugged – 'daft.'

'You said yourself you were threatened by a small child,' said Liam.

'That was just a wee boy playing soldiers!'

'Yes, with a lethal weapon.' Liam looked like he was thinking hard. 'You know ... I wonder what kind of education that kid is getting.'

'He can read,' I said.

Liam just smiled. 'I'll give this some thought,' he said. He glanced over at Kelly. 'Tab it in my diary?'

The secretary nodded.

Later that evening I saw Liam off in a corner of a corridor talking to himself. Then I realised he was talking on his phone. I hoped he was just calling home, but I knew I couldn't count on it.

10. MONDAY MORNING FEELING

I woke about seven just as it was getting light. But it wasn't the light that woke me. And my alarm hadn't gone off. I lay staring at the little red numbers on the clock stuck to the bunk above me and wondered what had woken me up. Then I heard it: a deep, distant throb, growing by the minute.

A helicopter. The sound always feels like a threat. Here comes a chopper to chop off your head.

I swung my legs off the bunk and sat up. Everybody else in the hut was still sound asleep. I padded to the door, went out quietly and looked around the side of the hut. I was freezing but I could see right along the loch. It was grey and still under a low ceiling of cloud. The chopper was a fat black drop heading straight towards me. Just as it passed level with the village it banked to my left and swung around to the south. It was one of those big two-engine Chinooks. A troop carrier.

The racket from it washed over the site. The chopper flew low over Strathcarron and skimmed the skyline. It disappeared behind the hills but I could still hear it. The chopper's heavy throb stayed steady. I guessed it was hovering.

'That's it for your bandits,' said Murdo, from behind me.

I turned. Like me he stood shivering in a vest and long johns, staring after the thing. I felt like giving the Lewisman a clout in his gloomy face. There's this with the Lewis folk, they expect the worst and are not often disappointed.

'Send soldiers after new age settlers?' I said. 'What are you on? It'll be just an exercise.'

Murdo shook his head.

'Don't kid yourself. You know fine what it's hovering over.' IIe snorted. 'I'm sure Social Services will be along in a while. Once the soldiers have secured the place.'

'I wish I'd kept my trap shut,' I said.

'You learn fast for a Glasgow boy,' said Murdo.

I wanted again to clout him but I just smacked my fist into my hand.

'We've got to *do* something!'

He gave me a funny look.

'We do, eh? Speak for yourself. But what can we do?'

'We can go up and see if we can help.'

'We can't fight the soldiers.'

'No, but we can maybe pick up anyone who gets away. Or help them to move their stuff.'

'That's possible,' Murdo said. 'I'll come along for the ride.'

I made a turn as if to dash for the truck. Murdo caught my shoulder.

'Get your clothes on,' he said. 'And take a piss first.'

Ten minutes later I was in the cab, Murdo and Euan beside me. Nobody was riding shotgun. Or maybe we all were, if you see what I mean. Euan was filling the air with his smoke, an early morning kick-start to his brain. I opened a window and turned up the heaters full blast. The sleepy security guard at the gate waved us out. He might have been a bit surprised when I turned left and took off towards Strathcarron.

We bumped across the tracks at the level crossing. I swung the truck to the left again, then right, up the old track. The wheels were off the track at both sides but the gripper tyres did their job all right.

'How far can we take it?' Euan asked, as we clawed up the first steep slope.

'Farther than this anyway,' I said.

The truck lurched down and forward. We bounced in our seats. I was worried about what lay ahead of us but I was enjoying this. A few minutes later we were nearly in the cloud. Then the cloud opened in a freezing drizzle that stung like sand. I closed the windows and switched on the wipers and headlights. The squeak and thud of the wipers took over as the loudest noise in the cab. We could see for about a hundred metres. Up and down we went, mostly up.

Then up and over and looking down into the glen where the settlement was. I stopped there, engine running, foot on the brake. We were leaning a long way forward. The chopper had landed right below us on the shore of the narrow loch, big and black against the strip of white ice.

A dozen or so soldiers in black armour suits

and visored helmets ringed the settlement. About the same number of the people who lived there stood on the track in a huddle. The greenhouses glittered with broken glass. Smoke, black and foul, rose from the two houses.

'Christ, man, they're burning the roofs!' said Murdo. He sounded choked. Euan banged a fist on the top of the dash. His face went as white and tight as his knuckles.

'Clearances,' he said. 'Clearances!'

He reached behind him for the shotgun on the rack. I grabbed his wrist and wrenched him away from it.

Two of the soldiers came racing up the slope towards us. They ran to either side of the truck, jumped on the running boards, and banged on the windows. I thumbed the roll-down switch. A visored face leaned in.

'Turn off the engine and get out of the cab now!'

'Right away,' I said.

The soldiers jumped back, and stood with their rifles pointed at us. I looked at the others.

'Well, boys,' I said. 'Time to go.'

We opened the doors. Murdo and Euan jumped

down from their side. I turned off the engine and jumped down from mine.

The truck was rolling forward before I hit the ground.

I swear I didn't plan this. I really was so rattled that I'd done exactly what the soldier had told me. I had turned off the engine and got out.

He never said anything about the handbrake.

The big Highway truck rolled down the slope. I heard yells, then I heard shots. For a moment it seemed like the soldiers thought they were dealing with a suicide bomber. Then I saw they were shooting at the tyres. I had just enough time to think this was a smart move.

The two front tyres blew out just as the front wheels went over the edge of the path, where it curved off at the shore of the loch in front of the houses. The nose of the truck slammed down. Oh aye, that bit stopped moving all right. The rest of the truck kept right on moving. The back of it rose into the air and seemed to hang there for a second. Then it toppled right over and crashed forward like a falling tree, right on to the chopper. The Chinook's fuel and the truck's electrics took a couple of seconds to find each other. Just as well, because everybody was flat on the ground when the fuel tank exploded. It wasn't the sort of explosion that hurls debris everywhere. It was a big blast of burning petrol vapour that scorched the back of my neck.

When I looked up the remains of the truck and the chopper were in the middle of one big mass of flame and smoke. It was like what you see on the television from Tehran any day. The soldiers ran towards it and stopped when the heat was too much. Then around the side of the burning wreckage came a dripping figure. It was the pilot, who must have jumped out and crashed through the ice of the loch when he saw the truck bearing down. I felt relieved about that.

I stood up and looked around and noticed that with all this commotion the people from the settlement had disappeared. They were off down the wee glen, then up the slopes like deer. I saw an officer peering after them through binoculars. Then he lowered the glasses and shook his head and pointed at us.

With that half the soldiers formed a cordon and walked up the hill towards us.

'Looks like we're for it now,' said Murdo.

'Run for it!' said Euan.

'Nae point,' I said. 'They'll shoot us.'

'Sounds like a plan,' said Murdo. But we weren't that desperate. Not then.

We raised our hands above our heads and waited for the boots and butts.

11. THE SECOND JIN YANG

The soldiers were maybe twenty metres away down the slope from us when I heard a strange whizzing sound and saw sparkles of light from the hillside opposite. Then a second later a sound came, a steady *did-did-did* ...

I threw myself flat on the grass. I watched six men spin and drop in front of me. Saw the others down by the lochside fall too. It was over in seconds. I lay with my hands clasped over my head and then stood up and puked.

Dark figures popped up on the hillside at the far side of the loch and began to walk down. Men, women, kids, about twenty in all, far more than I'd seen the day before. Two of them lugged a light machine gun. They were Martin and Angus. I had wondered why they hadn't been drafted. I was wrong. They had done their stint. And once you've been in the army, they told me later, it's not that hard to find a way to find the weapons. You can get it all on the black market.

But that was later.

What happened right then, while the kids were looting the dead, was that Ailiss walked up to us with her face all black and a rifle in her hand. Her grin was very white on her dirt-smeared face.

'That was *brilliant*!' she said. 'God above, you guys are heroes! Running the truck down on them like that!'

'It was him who had that idea,' said Murdo, pointing at me.

Ailiss gave me a dangerous hug, with the rifle still clutched in one hand.

I looked at Murdo and Euan. They looked back at me. I knew what they were thinking. We couldn't go away now. For a start, there was no way the gang here would let us go. For the very good reason that we would tell everything we knew. One way or another.

Like poor Jin Yang, the Chinese guy on the plane who was mistaken for a hijacker, I never meant to start a war. But I did. The war at home, the war of the veterans and settlers and evacuees and laggers. The war that rose as steadily as the sea level. The war we're still in. If I'd known what was going to happen, I might have walked away and taken my chances, even if it meant a bullet in the back. I don't know now, even after all these years. I for sure didn't know then. All I knew was that Ailiss was looking at me in a way nobody had ever looked at me before. Like she was *proud* of me.

Laggers, I thought. Too dumb tae draft. But not too feart tae fight.

'Aye,' I said. 'It was my idea.'

Published with this volume

WINNING THROUGH
Brian Irvine

In *Winning Through* Brian Irvine tells the
truth about his life as a footballer. From family
life in Airdrie we follow him as he realises his
boyhood dreams. He becomes an international
player with Aberdeen and Scotland. But he has
to cope with bad times, and worse, when he is
told he has a serious and possibly fatal illness.
Finally he has to come to terms with the end
of a long playing career. Brian's Christian faith
and strong family ties help him to cope,
and to 'win through'.

Brian Irvine was a professional footballer
with Falkirk, Aberdeen, Dundee and Ross
County. He represented Scotland nine times
before illness interrupted his career. When he
retired from playing he became Football
Development Officer with Ross County, a job
that includes community work in schools and
prison. He can often be heard giving
his expert comment on radio.

WICKED!
Janet Paisley

Jas overhears his wife in bed with an Italian.
His plan to retire early and spend their winters
in Italy is out the window. He tries to confront
Linda but it all goes wrong. Is she toying with
him? She's toying with lots of other things –
Italians, sexy underwear, massage oil. Jas tries
to end it all but that goes wrong too. Is his life
over? Or has he got the wrong end of the stick?
Just when things can't get worse, worse
is what they get.

Janet Paisley is the award-winning author of five
books of poetry, two fiction books and many
plays, radio, TV and film scripts. She grew up in
Avonbridge, near Falkirk, is the single parent of
six grown-up sons and is a first-time grannie.
Her writing is used in schools and universities in
Russia, Europe and America.

Also available

THE CHERRY SUNDAE COMPANY
Isla Dewar

THE BLUE HEN
Des Dillon

THE WHITE CLIFFS
Suhayl Saadi

BLOOD RED ROSES
Lin Anderson

GATO
Margaret Elphinstone

THESE TIMES, THIS PLACE
Muriel Gray

Moira Forsyth, *Series Editor for the Sandstone Vistas, writes:*

The Sandstone Vista Series of books has been developed for readers who are not used to reading full length novels, or for those who simply want to enjoy a 'quick read' which is satisfying and well written.